A Louis Louis Book

Louis goes to Edinburgh

For Andrew x

You may also enjoy

Louis finds a new home
ISBN 9780957027909

Louis goes to Brussels
ISBN 9780957027916

Louis goes to Paris
ISBN 9780957027954

A Louis Louis book
published by
wee dug books 2015

Author
Gillian Muir

Illustrator
Delphine Frantzen

Dog
Louis

When they arrived in Scotland,
Scottish granny was
very pleased to
meet Louis.
And Louis was very
pleased to meet
Scottish granny!

"Come on in for a cup of tea," she said.
Scottish granny never just had tea,
she had
potato scones,
fruit scones,
homemade shortbread
and tablet.

"Yum, yum!" thought Louis.

Soon the whole family arrived to meet Louis,
even Great Uncle Gordon who was
nearly a hundred years old.

Louis could hear chattering, laughter
and the clink clink clinking of tea cups.
"Time to head over to Edinburgh," said Dad.

"See you soon Louis!"

As they drove into the city
they parked beside a
strange looking building.

"Come on I've something
to show you!" said Mum.

They climbed up the stairs to
the back of the West Stand
to see the magnificent skyline of
Edinburgh from Murrayfield stadium.

"Look Louis, there's the castle.
It's built on an old volcano!"

"Are there any good shops in Edinburgh?"
asked the girl.
"Oh yes and so much more,"
replied Mum.

And she was right…

The city was alive.
The Edinburgh Festival
was in full swing.
Louis had never
seen anything like it!

At the top of the
Royal Mile they
came to the castle.

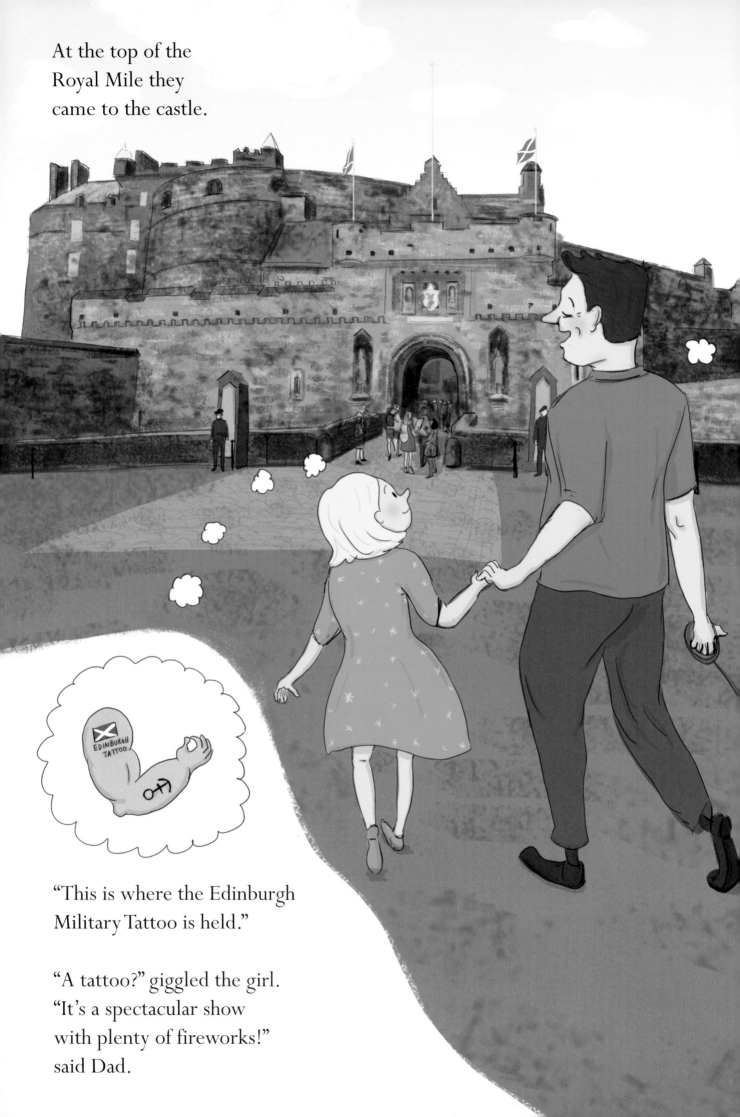

"This is where the Edinburgh
Military Tattoo is held."

"A tattoo?" giggled the girl.
"It's a spectacular show
with plenty of fireworks!"
said Dad.

But Louis was not happy.
He had heard a very strange
wailing noise.

It got louder and **louder**…

It was a piper getting ready
to play his bagpipes!

A crowd started to gather.
They tapped their feet
to the music and
Louis wagged his
little brown tail.

From the castle they
could see for miles.

"You two stay here for a moment!" said Dad.

Then suddenly...

BANG!

The children
jumped up
in the air.
Louis barked!
"Don't worry,"
said Mum.

WAF
WAF

"It's the one o'clock gun!
It's fired everyday, except Sundays.
Everyone in Edinburgh knows
when it is one o'clock."

They wound their way down the cobbled
streets to the Grassmarket.
They took different routes.
"Louis Louis!" called the boy.
When Louis saw them he
peeked his head through the railings.

"Come on down Louis!"

"We want you to meet a
very famous wee Edinburgh dog."

"Here he is!"

Louis looked up at the statue.

"He's called Greyfriar's Bobby.
He was a very
loyal dog,
just like
you Louis."

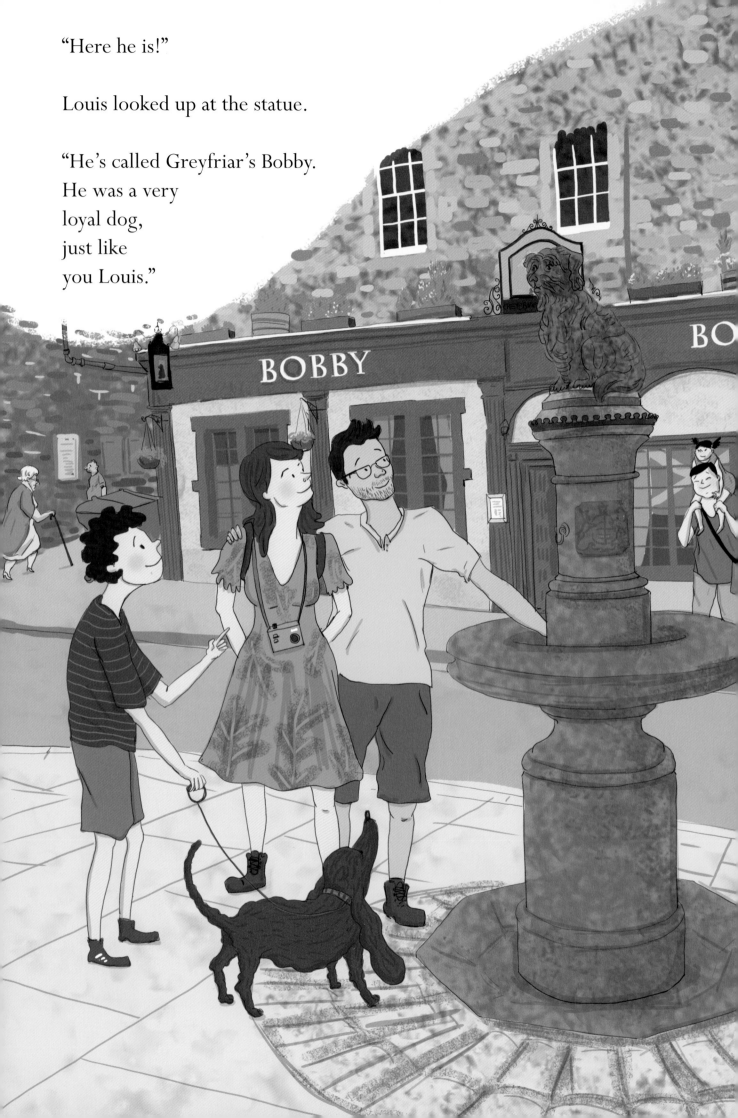

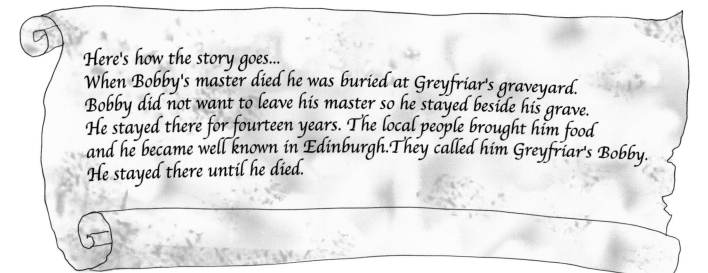

Here's how the story goes...
When Bobby's master died he was buried at Greyfriar's graveyard.
Bobby did not want to leave his master so he stayed beside his grave.
He stayed there for fourteen years. The local people brought him food
and he became well known in Edinburgh. They called him Greyfriar's Bobby.
He stayed there until he died.

"Let's go into the graveyard and
take a look around."

There was a sign that said
no dogs allowed.
They looked a little closer and saw
what someone had written on the sign.

It made them laugh.

NO DOGS
MANAGEMENT RULES

- ———————
- ———————
- ———————
- ———————

THESE RULES WILL NOT APPLY
TO GUIDE DOGS OR POLICE DOGS AND BOBBY!

GREYFRIARS BOBBY
DIED 14TH JANUARY 1872
AGED 16 YEARS

LET HIS LOYALTY & DEVOTION
BE A LESSON TO US ALL

As they twisted back under archways,
through closes and along cobbled streets
they stopped to admire the
view of Princes Street.

"Look Louis, shops on one side
and gardens on the other.
There's something for everyone!"

They even
caught their
first glimpse of
an Edinburgh tram.

They stopped to admire the gardens.
"Time to hit the shops!" said Dad.
But Louis had other plans.

He tug tug tugged
on his lead.

"Why do you want to
go into the gardens Louis?"

Louis had spotted squirrels.
They were tame and
not afraid of people at all.
They were very persistent squirrels.

They wanted **lunch!**

WAF
WAF
WAF

They watched
and chuckled.

But Louis was not happy.
He wanted to chase
the squirrels!

After coaxing Louis away from the squirrels,
they hopped on a tram.
Louis sat and watched
the world glide by.

Off they hopped
and after a short walk
they arrived…

at Edinburgh Zoo
just in time for the penguin parade!

Then back to the city centre
and off they headed to…

the hustle and bustle of Stockbridge!
It was full of interesting
little shops.

"What a cute wee dog.
His coat is so soft
like a teddy bear!"

After shopping they walked alongside the Water of Leith. Louis had a good old bark at the ducks!

"Come on Louis this way!"

"Let's go to Grandad's favourite street in Edinburgh. A painter called Henry Raeburn designed the street and named it after his wife. Can you spot anything unusual about this street?" said Mum.

"Hey, I see that the houses have front gardens and both sides of the street look the same. Like a mirror image!"

Louis trotted up the street looking from side to side.

They headed back into the city
and stopped to look at the
amazing Scottish Parliament building.

"Look at all the different
styles of buildings. Did you
know that Edinburgh is
sometimes called the
Athens of the North?"

They crossed a busy road.
Louis stuck his head through
the gates of Holyrood Palace.

"Are you hoping
to catch a glimpse
of the royal family, Louis?"
giggled the girl.

They then started the
steep climb up to an old
volcano called Arthur's Seat.

Stopping for a rest they
admired the wonderful
view across the city.

"Edinburgh is such a beautiful city,
erupting with great things to see and do!"
announced the boy.

They all agreed.

However Louis wasn't listening.
He was fast asleep,
probably dreaming of chasing
the Princes Street garden squirrels!

Where will Louis go next?